"Where does madness leave off and reality begin?"

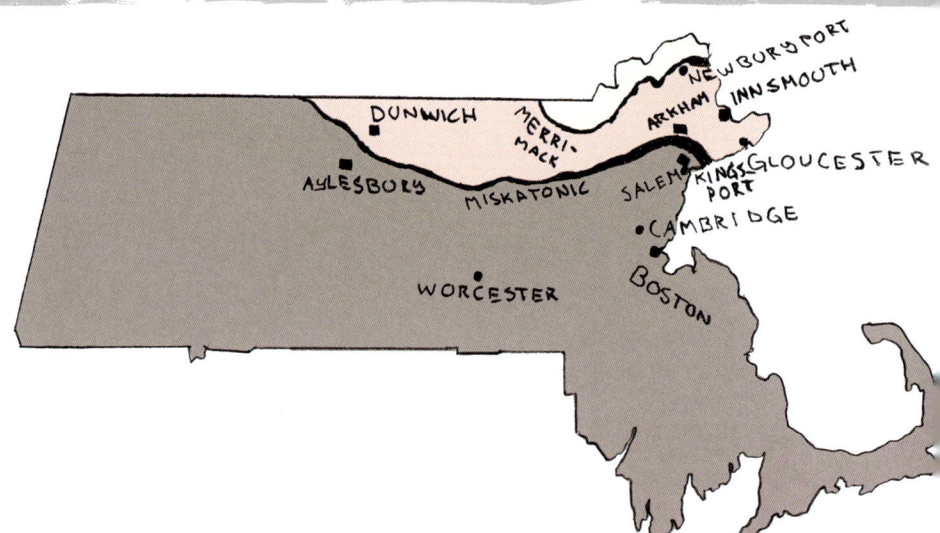

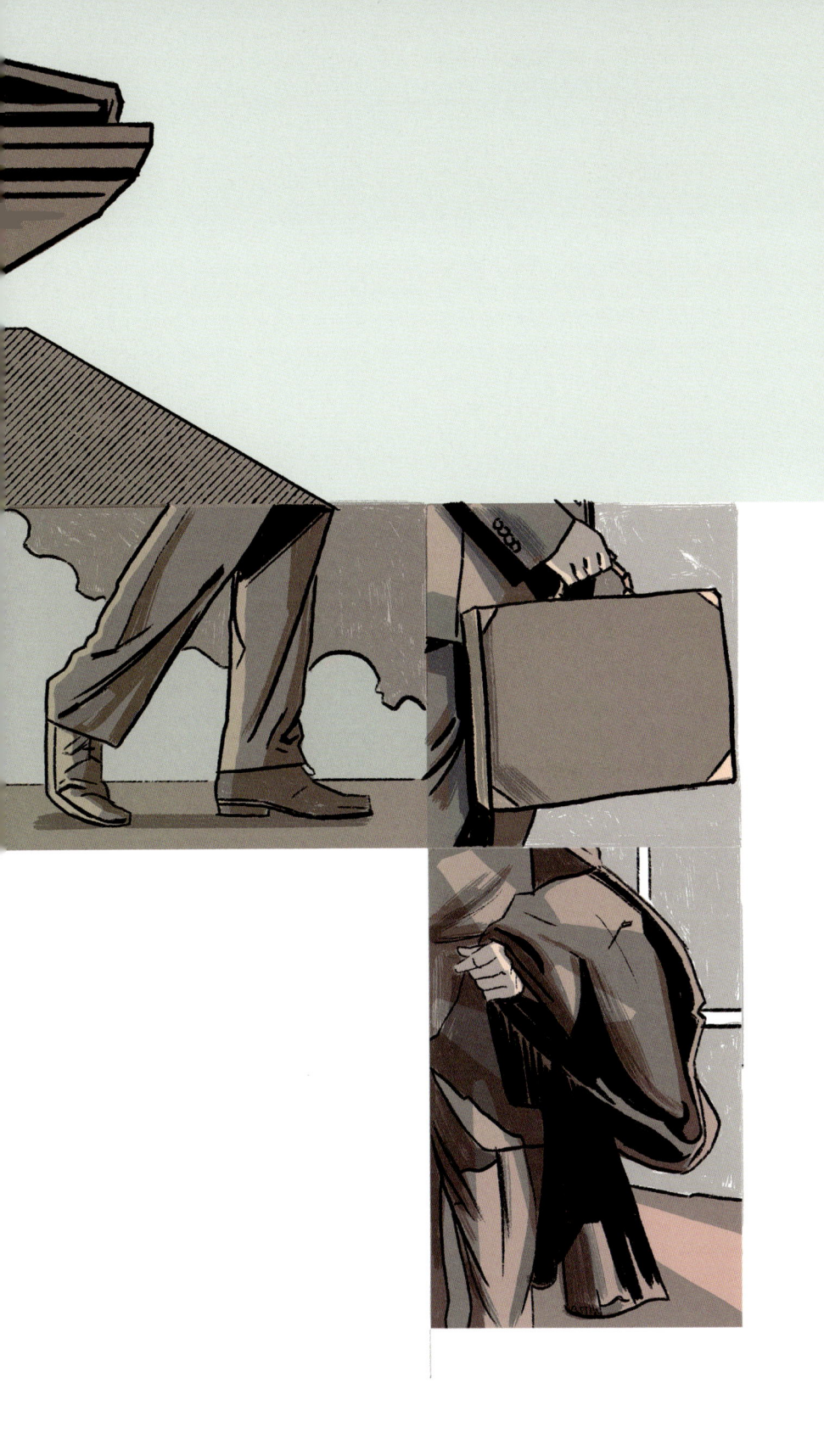

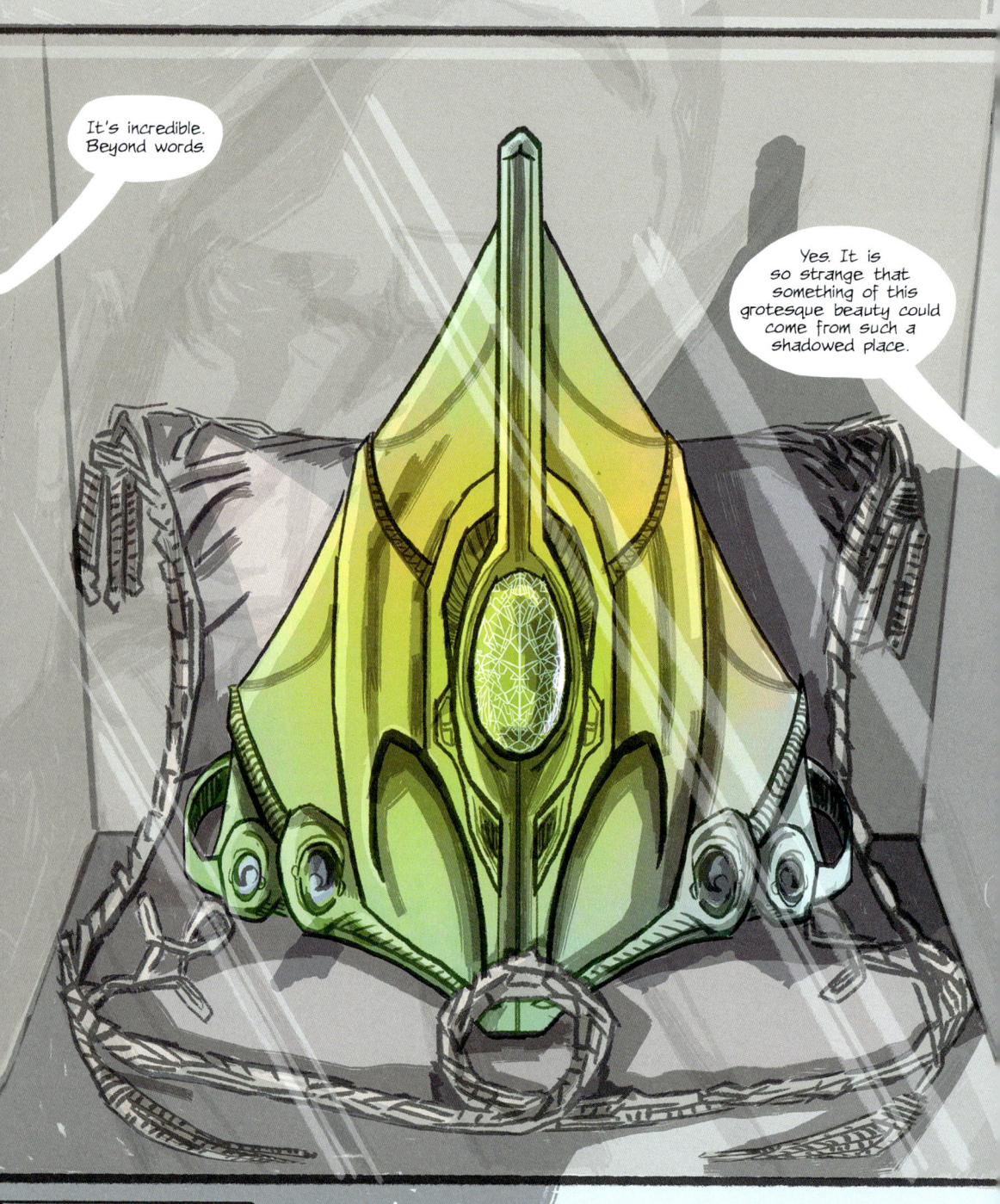

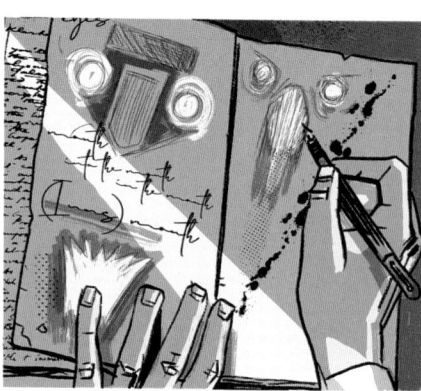

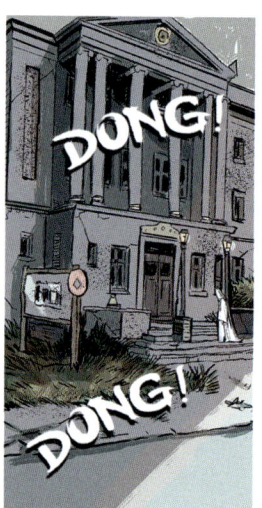

GGUUURRGLE

Ah, the fire station.

"You have brought what we needed?"

"And more besides, Walekea."

"Very well. Come speak with me tonight."

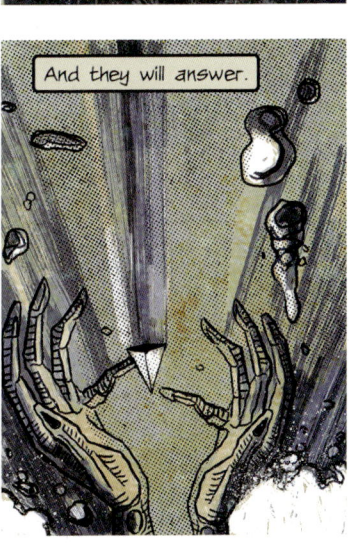

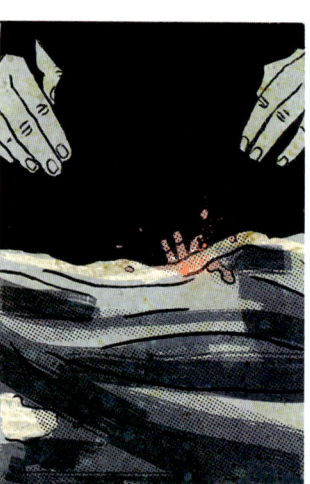

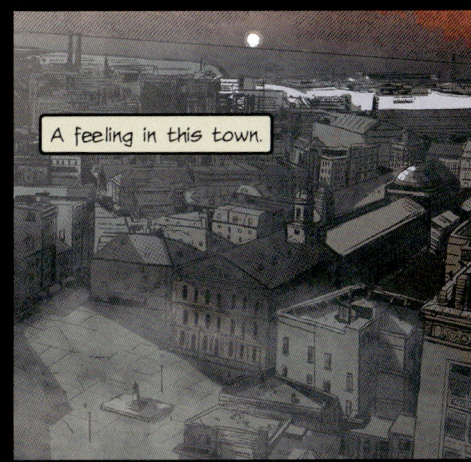

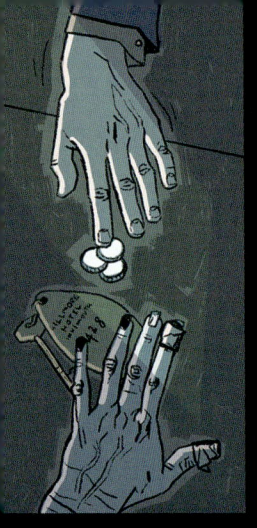

Hmph. It'll do.

For one night.

No lock.

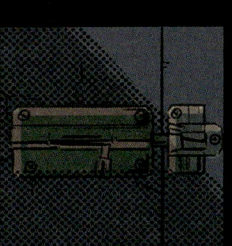

I can't hear them.

And there's a breeze...

...coming through here.

Outside, at last.

10.35.

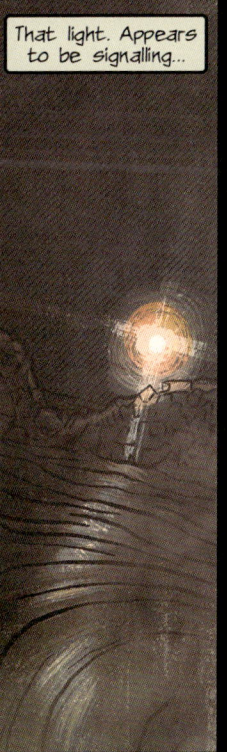

 But that's all I need.

 Ignore what you see.

 Shut it out.

 Fear will kill me if I let it.

I am one against many.

But I will survive.

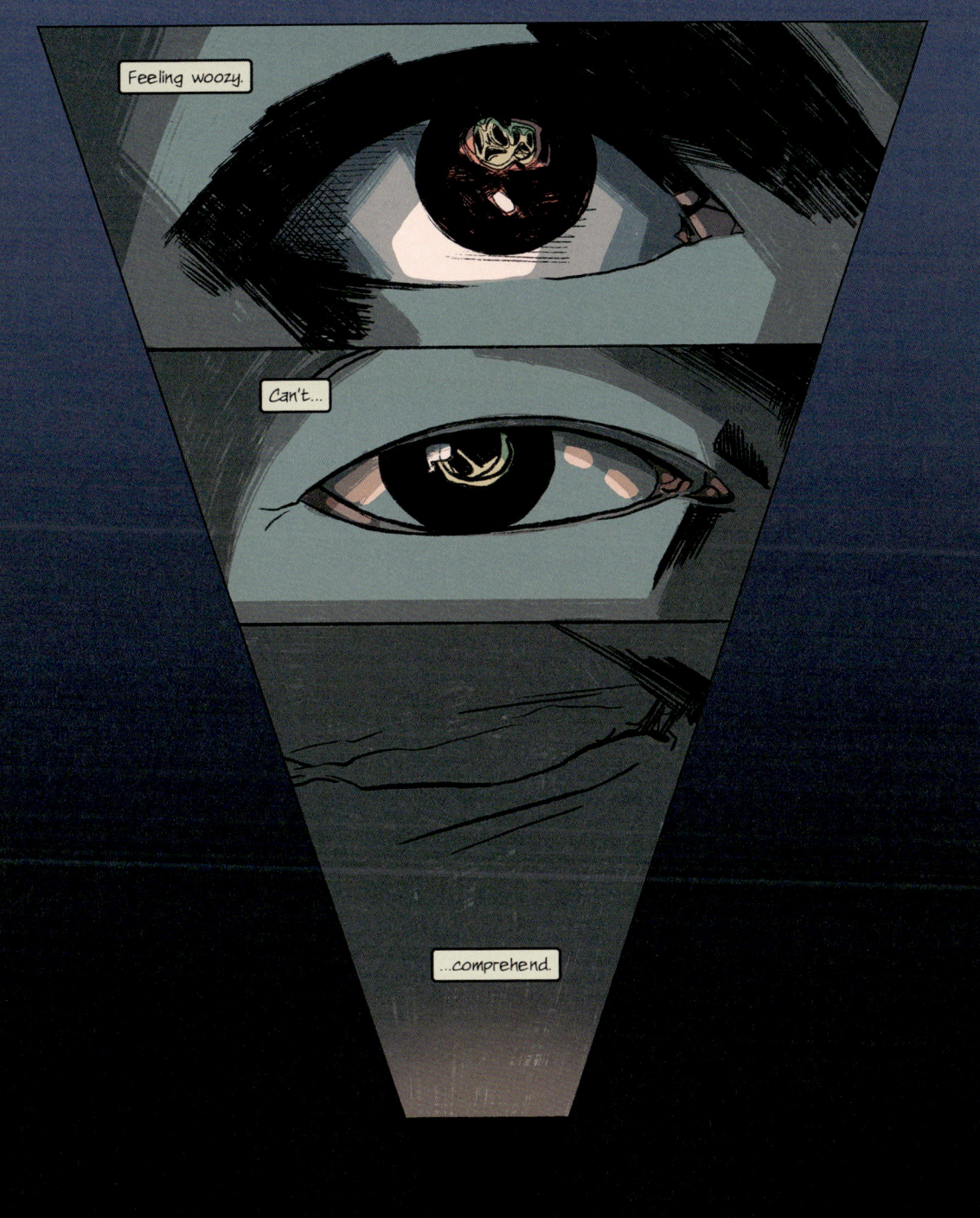

A few months later, they acted.

A few months later...

...I was researching my lineage...

...to ensure I had nothing...

...to do with them.

Capt. Obed Marsh

Alice Marsh

Eliza Orne (Arkham)

Robert Olmstead

There were indescribable creatures.

And bottomless levels.

Still, I descended the steps.

And faced the entities there.

And they looked back at me.

COVER GALLERY

THE SHADOW OVER INNSMOUTH

PART TWO: ORIGINS OF INNSMOUTH

BIRKS   RHSTEWART   WHITE

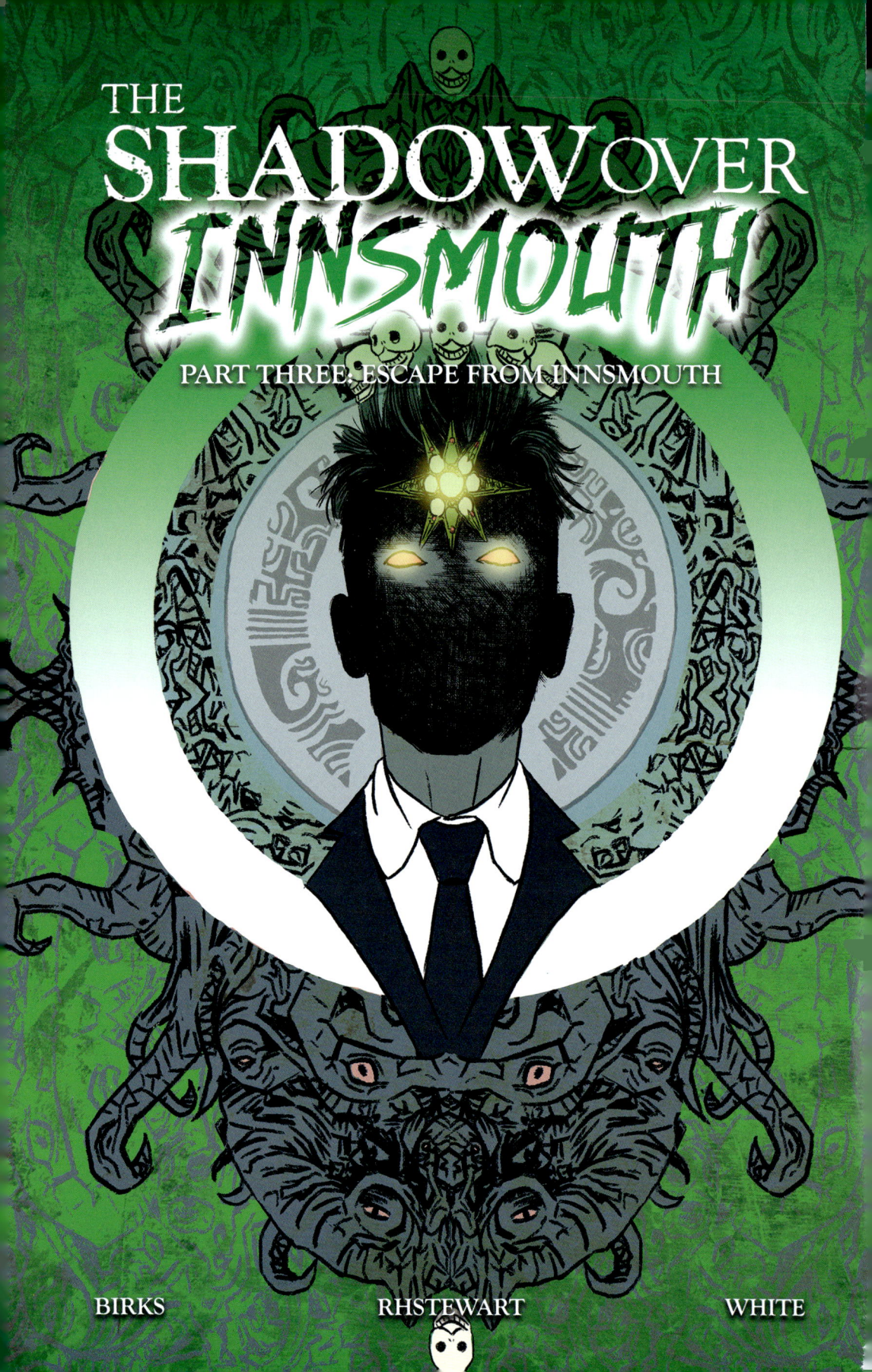